Calico Cat
at the Zoo

written and illustrated by Donald Charles

ℚ CHILDRENS PRESS, CHICAGO

for the potter smiths

Library of Congress Cataloging in Publication Data

Charles, Donald.
  Calico Cat at the zoo.

  SUMMARY: Calico Cat visits various animals in the
zoo, characterizing them as big, quiet, proud, funny, and
many other adjectives.
  1. Vocabulary—Juvenile literature. [1. English
language—Adjective. 2. English language—Synonyms
and antonyms. 3. Vocabulary] I. Title.
PE1449.C43   5   428.1   80-25380
ISBN 0-516-03443-X

Calico Cat
at the Zoo

Calico Cat is going
to the zoo
to see the animals.

4

big

6

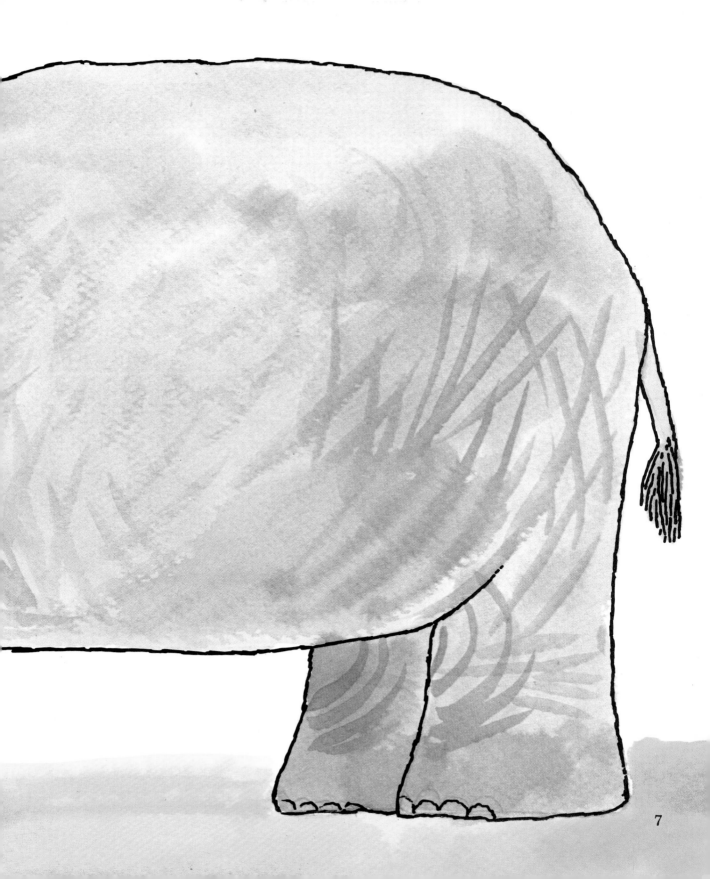

7

small

short

tall

12

13

14

shy

proud

quiet

gentle

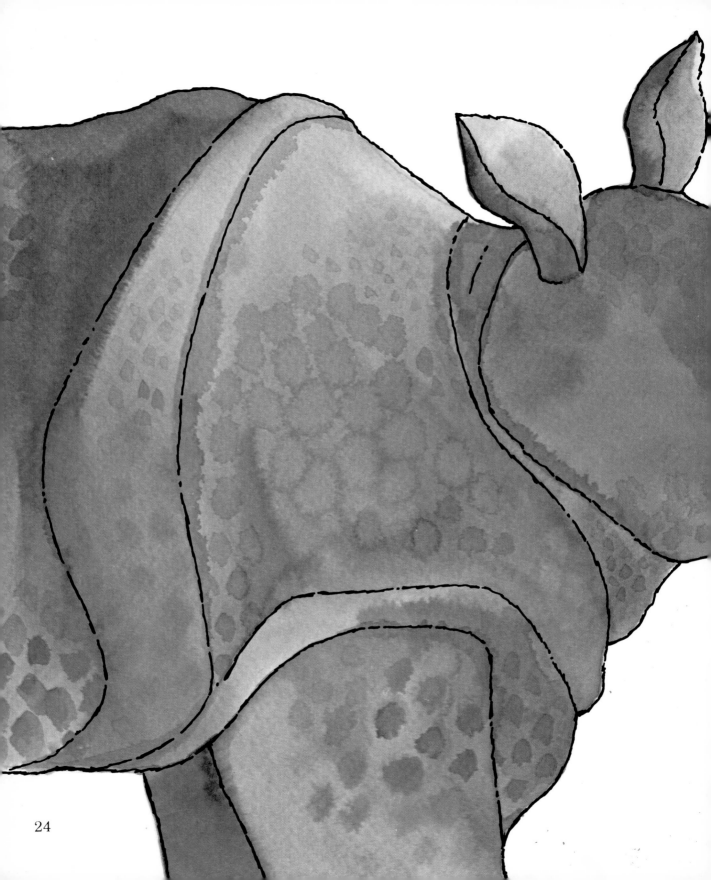

mean

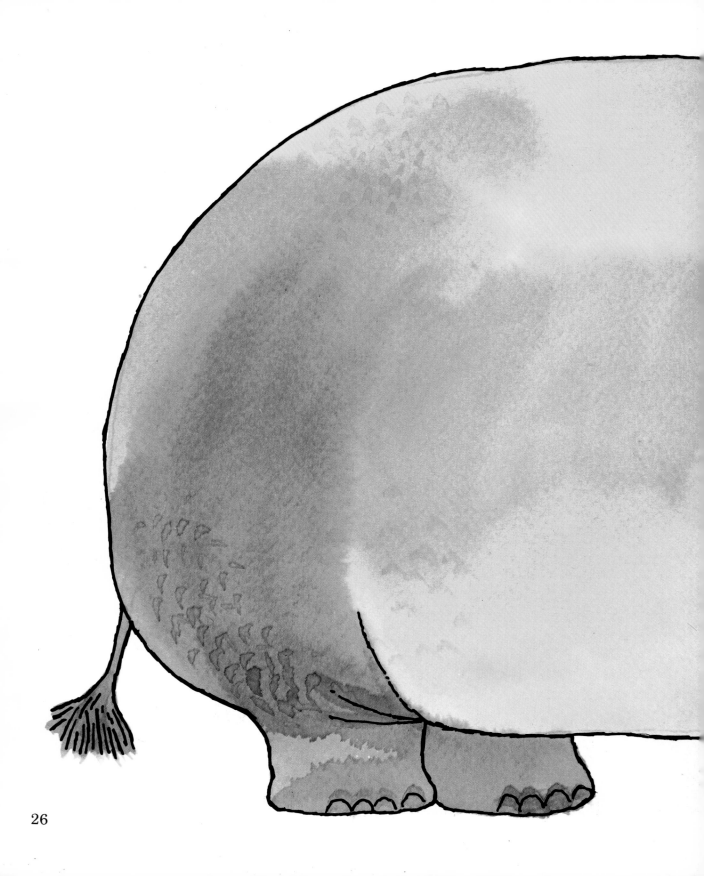

fat

lean

and funny!

Calico Cat can name the animals.
Can you?

elephant

hedgehog

turtle

giraffe

gorilla

lion

zebra

parrot

deer

rhino

hippo

snake

monkey

ABOUT THE AUTHOR/ARTIST

Donald Charles started his long career as an artist and author more than twenty-five years ago after attending the University of California and the Art League School of California. He began by writing and illustrating feature articles for the *San Francisco Chronicle,* and also sold cartoons and ideas to *The New Yorker* and *Cosmopolitan* magazines. Since then he has been, at various times. a longshoreman, ranch hand, truck driver, and editor of a weekly newspaper, all enriching experiences for a writer and artist. Ultimately he became creative director for an advertising agency, a post which he resigned several years ago to devote himself full-time to book illustration and writing. Mr. Charles has received frequent awards from graphic societies, and his work has appeared in numerous textbooks and periodicals.